This book belongs to

_____

_____

To Luther, Jack, Daisy and Flory

J.W.

First published in 2007 in Great Britain by Gullane Children's Books
This paperback edition published in 2008 by
Gullane Children's Books
185 Fleet Street, London, EC4A 2HS
www.gullanebooks.com

1   3   5   7   9   10   8   6   4   2

Text and illustrations © Jude Wisdom 2007

The right of Jude Wisdom to be identified as the author and
illustrator of this work has been asserted by her in accordance
with the Copyright, Designs, and Patents Act, 1988.

A CIP record for this title is available from the British Library.

ISBN: 978-1-86233-723-7

Printed and bound in Indonesia

Billy
Jupiter

Jude
Wisdom

GULLANE
CHILDREN'S BOOKS

Billy Jupiter often felt afraid. He lived all on his
own in a packet of Spaceflakes. He was frightened of the
dark and the strange crackly noises the Spaceflakes made
whenever he tried to move. He sometimes wondered what
life would be like outside the packet, but was
too scared to think about it much.

'Mind you,' he said to himself one day,
'It can't get much worse than this!' Suddenly . . .

The packet was opened and the
Spaceflakes were poured into a bowl.

Out bounced Billy who pinged
off a plate, and . . .

. . . landed on the floor with a SPLAT!

He leapt up, sped
across the kitchen . . .

hopped through
the cat-flap, and . . .

. . . found himself running through gigantic flowers
as fast as his little green legs could carry him!

He hadn't gone far when he came across
a group of bugs. 'Hello,' called a ladybird.
'Welcome to the village!' beamed
an elderly caterpillar.

Billy Jupiter stopped and stared.
He was too scared to speak, but
nobody seemed to notice.

'Come closer!' growled a beetle, beckoning to Billy with a long blue
finger. 'The sun is going down and the moon will soon be up!'
'What do you mean?' asked Billy Jupiter with a stutter.
'SHE will soon be here,' said the beetle.

Billy Jupiter didn't like the sound of this at all –
he wished he were back in the Spaceflakes.

'As soon as the moon is up,' the beetle went on,
'out she comes. SHE is the biggest, hairiest . . .

SPIDER!

And she skulks around outside the village . . .'
'We all know what she wants!' wailed the ladybird.
'She wants to weave us all into her
web – then gobble us up for tea!'
She began to sob loudly.

'Cheer up, Ladybird!' said an excited baby earthworm. 'Now all our worries are over – Billy Jupiter is here to save the day!'

'Hurray!' shouted everyone.

'May I have your autograph?' asked the ladybird, wiping away a dewy tear, 'I've never met a real Superhero!'

'But I'm not a Superhero,' said Billy Jupiter.

'Nonsense, dear boy!' bellowed the elderly caterpillar. 'Allow me to show you something!'

He led the way to a large house made from a packet of Spaceflakes.
On it, was an enormous picture of Billy Jupiter scaring a gigantic
monster away with his space-zapper. In big, bold letters it said:
SUPERHERO BILLY JUPITER SAVES THE DAY!

Billy Jupiter couldn't believe his eyes. 'That can't be me,' he gasped.
'No time to waste now, Billy!' cried the elderly caterpillar. 'The moon
will be up at any minute – let's think of a plan!'
But it was too late . . .

A great gloomy shadow
fell across the village . . .
It was the Huge Hairy Spider!
Everyone ran and hid behind a
flower. Except for Billy Jupiter.
He was too frightened
to move.

'Isn't he BRAVE!'
gasped the ladybird.
'Seems to be shaking a
bit . . .' muttered the beetle.

Billy Jupiter stared at
the spider's great yellow
eyes and giant spindly legs.
She looked very hungry!

'USE YOUR SPACE-ZAPPER!' shouted the baby earthworm.
Billy tried to aim the space-zapper, but he couldn't stop shaking.
The Huge Hairy Spider began to speak . . .

'Excuse me!' she said politely,
'would you mind pointing that
thing in the other direction!'

'But you're about to gobble
us all up!' cried Billy Jupiter.

The spider looked shocked.
'Oh dearie me!' she said. 'What
a terrible thought! I'm only here
to look at the pretty lights because
I'm . . . I'm afraid of the dark!'

Billy Jupiter was amazed!
He didn't know what to say . . .

The spider waved at the others, who were still hiding behind the flower. They felt a little foolish, and wondered why they had ever felt so afraid of her!

'Welcome to the village!'
said the ladybird. 'This is
a wonderful place to live!'

And they all decided there
should be a party to celebrate
meeting their two special
new friends . . .

'I've never met a real Superhero!'
said the spider to Billy.

'But I don't feel like one!
I'm always frightened . . .'

'Don't be silly, Billy! Everybody's scared
of something!' said the big spider.

'Yes indeed. Life can be tough,
whether you're big or small!' said
the elderly caterpillar. 'But you
can still live happily ever after!'

And that's exactly what they did!

Other Gullane Children's Books for you to enjoy . . .

The Lamb-a-roo
written by
Diana Kimpton
illustrated by
Rosalind Beardshaw

The Smallest Hero
written by
Gillian Rogerson
illustrated by
Ingela Peterson

Billy Bean's Dream
written and illustrated by
Simone Lia

Blame it on the Great Blue Panda!
written by
Claire Freedman
illustrated by
Emma Carlow & Trevor Dickinson

Tabitha's Terrifically Tough Tooth
written and illustrated by
Charlotte Middleton